The Case for
Edward de Vere
as the real
WILLIAM SHAKESPEARE

The Case for
Edward de Vere
as the real
WILLIAM SHAKESPEARE

John Milnes Baker

The Case for Edward de Vere as the Real William Shakespeare
Copyright © 2024 by John Milnes Baker. All rights reserved.

No part of this publication may be reproduced, stored in a retrieval system or transmitted in any way by any means, electronic, mechanical, photocopy, recording or otherwise without the prior permission of the author except as provided by USA copyright law.

The opinions expressed by the author are not necessarily those of URLink Print and Media.

1603 Capitol Ave., Suite 310 Cheyenne, Wyoming USA 82001
1-888-980-6523 | admin@urlinkpublishing.com

URLink Print and Media is committed to excellence in the publishing industry.

Book design copyright © 2024 by URLink Print and Media. All rights reserved.

Published in the United States of America

Library of Congress Control Number: 2023922219
ISBN 978-1-68486-627-4 (Paperback)
ISBN 978-1-68486-628-1 (Hardback)
ISBN 978-1-68486-629-8 (Digital)

09.01.24

The Case for

Edward de Vere

as the real

WILLIAM SHAKESPEARE

A Challenge to Conventional Wisdom

John Milnes Baker

Why do so many people question the authorship of Shakespeare's works? The answer may be found in this booklet and the references on pages 34 and 35.

Acknowledgments
First my thanks to all the writers on pages 34 and 35.

I have chosen to omit footnotes for my many assertions in this elementary introduction to the Shakespeare Authorship Question. But all points are expounded by these writers with appropriate scholarly references and documentation.

I am indebted to Joseph Hanaway, MD, CM, FAAN for his helpful suggestions in editing this booklet. He has been skeptical of the Stratfordian narrative since his days at McGill University.

Kate Delano-Condax Decker is a writer and an insightful wordsmith. Her suggestions were always spot on.

I must also thank Alex McNeil, editor of *The Shakespeare Oxford Newsletter*, for his valued comments and informative suggestions.

This book was designed and illustrated by the author. The maps and drawings are original and any people depicted in stock imagery provided by Getty Images are models. And such images are being used for illustrative purposes only. Certain stock imagery © Getty Images.

Note:

Cover portrait the Earl of Oxford: "A 17th -century portrait based on lost 1575 original. National Portrait Gallery, London" --- WikipediA

The de Vere Coat of Arms
The boar was the heraldic device of the earls of Oxford, It is depicted as the crest within a wreath atop the helmet.
Motto: VERO NIHIL VERIUS (Nothing is Truer than Truth)

To all who have explored the
Shakespeare Authorship Coalition's
Declaration of Reasonable Doubt About
the Identity of William Shakespeare
www.DoubtAboutWill.org

PRELIMINARY NOTES
Terminology and some helpful clarifications:

The distinction between the two persons in the "Shakespeare Authorship Question." (SAQ)

Will(iam) **Shakspere** (1564-1616)
The reputed author from Stratford-upon-Avon

William Shakespeare
The pen name of Edward de Vere, seventeenth Earl of Oxford (1550-1604) (aka: *Edward*, *Oxford* and *de Vere*)

Stratfordian
A proponent of Will Shakspere of Stratford-upon-Avon as the purported author William Shakespeare

Oxfordian
Someone who believes Edward de Vere was the author of the works attributed to William Shakespeare

First Folio (1623)
The first collection of William Shakespeare's works contained thirty-six plays. Subsequently two more have been acknowledged by most scholars as Shakespeare's:
The Two Noble Kinsmen and *Pericles, Prince of Tyre*.

Mon**u**ment vs. Mon**i**ment
(Note the ambiguity in the introduction to the First Folio)

Monument generally refers to an actual stone, statue or building erected in remembrance of a person or event.

Moniment (archaic) implies "a collection of documents."

Dating of the plays
The dating of the plays has long been a subject of disagreement among both Stratfordians and Oxfordians. Many early versions were revised by the author from time to time making the dating conjectural at best. Some plays may have even been reworked by others after de Vere's death.

CONTENTS

Preface vii

1 Who was Edward de Vere? 1

2 Edward's Early Years 13

3 Married Life 17

4 Edward's Later Life 23

5 After Edward's Death 27

Postscript 36

Note:
The references on pages 34 and 35 provide the reader with the background for the subject of this

"Challenge to Conventional Wisdom"

Also, I encourage anyone not familiar with the Oxfordian view, but curious to explore the subject, to visit the following websites:

https://shakespeareoxfordfellowship.org

https://www.deveresociety.co.uk

https://doubtaboutwill.org

(The Shakespeare Authorship Coalition's "Declaration of Reasonable Doubt")

Comments by some distinguished doubters:

I am haunted by the conviction that the divine William is the biggest and most successful fraud ever practiced on a patient world.   - Henry James

The long interval during which Shakespeare's writings lay in comparative neglect has spread its own shadow over his history. And it is his good and evil lot that scarcely anything remains to his biographers but a scanty handful of conjectures.
                    - Washington Irving

There is nothing preserved of this great genius which is worth knowing. Nothing which might inform us of what education, what company, what accident turned his mind to letters and the drama.   - John Adams

I no longer believe that William Shakespeare the actor from Stratford was the author of the works ascribed to him.
                    - Sigmund Freud

It is my final belief that the Shakesperean plays were written by another hand than Shaksper's [sic] .... I do not seem to have any patience with the Shaksper argument: it is all gone for me – up the spout. The Shaksper case is about closed.
                    - Walt Whitman

*The strange, difficult, contradictory man who emerges as **the real Shakespeare**, Edward de Vere, the 17th Earl of Oxford, is not just plausible but fascinating and wholly believable. It's hard to imagine anyone reading the book with an open mind ever seeing Shakespeare or his works in the same way again.*

                    - David McCullough
                    From the foreword to Charlton Ogburn's
                    The Mysterious William Shakespeare

Note: And the list could go on: Ralph Waldo Emerson, Orson Welles, Oliver Wendell Holmes, John Galsworthy, Charlie Chaplin, James Joyce, Nathaniel Hawthorne, Benjamin Disraeli, William James, Sir John Gielgud, Clifton Fadiman, and many more.

Preface

William Shakespeare, the "Bard of Stratford-on-Avon," has long been considered the greatest writer in the Western World. But who was the real "William Shakespeare"?

Was it the Stratford man named Will Shakspere (*pronounced **shax-pur***), reputed actor, member of a theater troupe, a minor shareholder in the Globe theater and a moneylender from Stratford-upon-Avon?

Or was "William Shakespeare" a pseudonym for a highly educated, well traveled courtier who chose to remain anonymous? That is the essence of the persistent "Shakespeare Authorship Question."

This "Challenge to Conventional Wisdom" is an elementary introduction to the authorship controversy espousing the case for Edward de Vere, the 17th Earl of Oxford, as the real William Shakespeare.

Disclaimer:

I am by no means a Shakespearean scholar – simply a lover of the plays.

However, I find the controversy fascinating and I encourage anyone reading this booklet to explore the extensive literature on the subject.

South Kent CT

Map of the British Isles

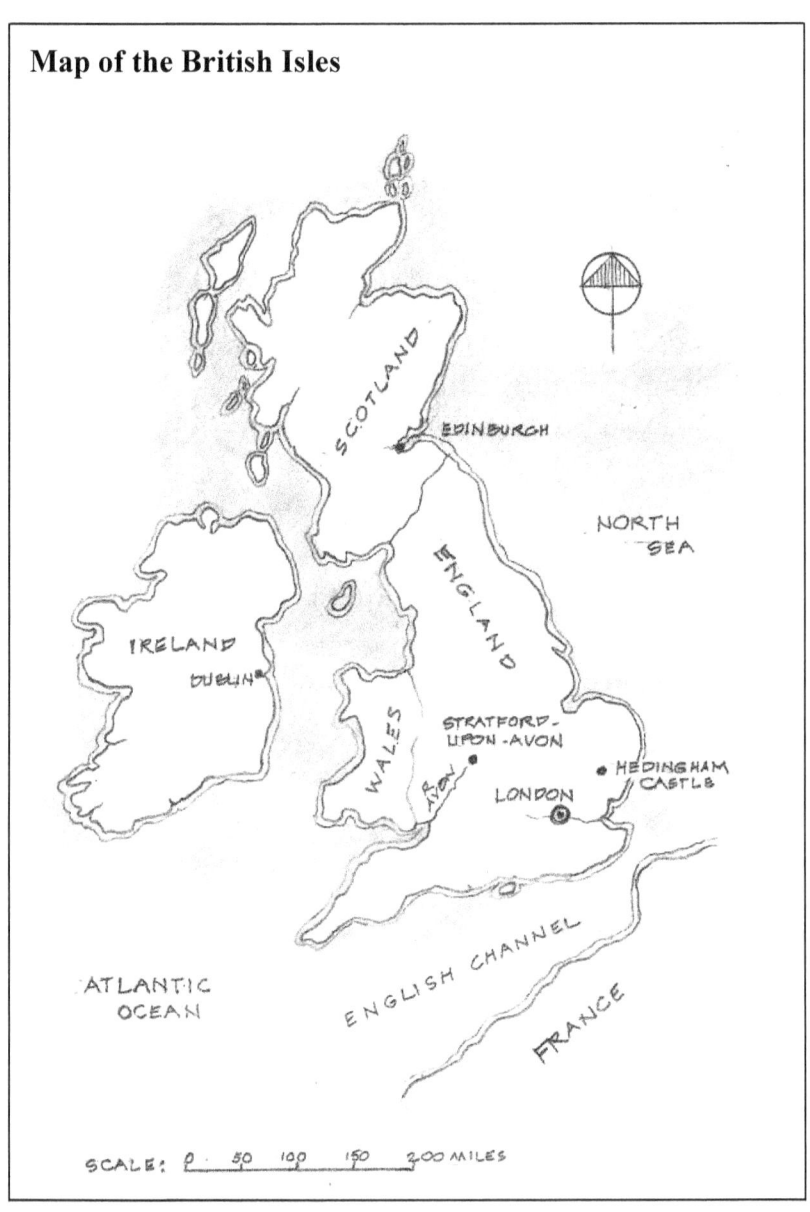

There were no permanent colonies established in British North America under Queen Elizabeth I. The Virginia Company of London was created in 1606 and the first permanent English colony was Jamestown, Virginia, established in 1607.

1 WHO WAS EDWARD DE VERE?

Edward de Vere was an Elizabethan aristocrat. He was the seventeenth Earl of Oxford and, as Lord Great Chamberlain, the highest ranking nobleman in England at that time. An ever increasing number of people have come to believe that he was also the actual playwright known as **"William Shakespeare."**

How can that be? Wasn't William Shakespeare, "The Bard of Stratford-on-Avon," the famous author? "Shakespeare" has indeed been considered the most gifted writer of the Western World for over four hundred years. There are innumerable orthodox biographies espousing the theory that Will Shakspere of Stratford-upon-Avon was the playwright William Shakespeare. But all invariably depend on conjecture unsupported by substantive documentary evidence.

There has been an ongoing debate for well over two hundred years about whether the reputed author,

Mark Twain never believed the Stratfordian myth and likened the notion to the "colossal skeleton brontosaur in the museum, with its nine bones and six-hundred barrels of plaster of Paris." In 1909, in his *Is Shakespeare Dead?*, the author of *Tom Sawyer* and *Huckleberry Finn* said he would ask debaters only one question. "Was Shakespeare ever a practicing lawyer? And leave everything else out."

Though the term "Stratfordian" hadn't been coined in 1909, that's whom Twain meant when he wrote:
"Those thugs have built their entire superstition upon *inferences*, not upon known and established facts."
and:
"The thug is aware that loudness convinces sixty persons where reasoning convinces but one."

Samuel Langhorne Clemens (1835-1910)
wrote under the pen name **Mark Twain**.

"Mark Twain" was a Mississippi riverboat pilot's term indicating a depth of two fathoms – twelve feet. That meant "Safe Water" – sufficient depth for riverboats.

Will Shakspere of Stratford-upon-Avon, could possibly have been the playwright. (That's how it was spelled, without the *e* in the middle and no *a* in *spear*.) Orthodox academics have endorsed the Stratfordian candidate for generations and do so today with exasperation with anyone who questions their assertions.

But it is not that simple: Over the years questions have been raised to challenge the Stratfordian account. **Walt Whitman**, **Mark Twain,** and **Sigmund Freud** are prominent among the numerous writers, scholars and historians who reject the Stratfordian theory. Even five Supreme Court justices: Harry Blackmun, John Paul Stevens, Lewis Powell, Antonin Scalia and Sandra Day O'Connor all weighed in on the controversy – all favored someone other than Will Shakspere of Stratford.

Numerous alternative candidates have been proposed, but since 1920, when an English school teacher named J. Thomas Looney published a book titled *"Shakespeare" Identified in Edward de Vere, the Seventeenth Earl of Oxford,* there has been only one

Who Was William Shakspere? (1564-1616)

William Shakspere (*pronounced **shax-pur***) was the son of John Shakspere of Stratford-upon-Avon, a small rural town approximately ninety miles northwest of London. Only about 2,000 people lived there and very few could even write their own names. Less than 5% of the population of the entire country were literate. Even many town fathers signed their names with an X.

Young Will *supposedly* attended the local grammar school where he *supposedly* studied Latin and classical literature. There is no proof that this was the case, and judging from the six signatures on page 8, he must not have learned to write.

In 1582, when he was eighteen, he married Anne Hathaway, eight years his senior, and they soon had three children. Sometime before 1592 he *supposedly* left for London leaving his family behind. The period from 1585 to 1592 is known as "Shakespeare's Lost Years" when there is no mention of the purported author in any record anywhere.

Will Shakspere *supposedly* had a career as an actor, theater manager, moneylender, and in 1599 was a minor shareholder in the Globe theater. In 1597 he bought New Place, the second largest house in Stratford. He *supposedly* left London for good and returned to his hometown around 1610. He *supposedly* retired from writing plays about 1612 but continued to sue people for paltry sums.

He died a wealthy man in New Place in 1616 and in his exhaustive will left most of his estate to his daughter Susanna but "his second best bed" to his widow.

And that's about it!   The rest is supposition.

*The family name was **Shakspere** – never **Shakespeare**! The two are NOT interchangeable. Stratfordians spell Will Shakspere as if he was known during his lifetime as William Shakespeare.   He was not.*
(See *Shakespeare Oxford Newsletter*, Fall 2022, page 24 - *JMB*/& *JH*)

serious contender with a convincing claim to the authorship. That person is Edward de Vere, the 17th Earl of Oxford (1550-1604).

The notion that Will Shakspere (1564-1616) of Stratford-upon-Avon was the author of the plays was not imagined until seven years after the Stratford man died. The First Folio of the collected works was published in 1623. In his introductory verses, Ben Jonson praised the "Sweet Swan of Avon" and Leonard Digges, in a separate poem, referred to the "Stratford Moniment." Stratfordians claim that these two quips combine to prove the connection of the Avon and Stratford to Shakespeare. This was the first time anyone suggested a connection between Will Shakspere and the plays of "William Shakespeare."

(Note that Ben Jonson was cagey, and certainly ambiguous, in hinting that "Avon" was associated with de Vere. The earl actually owned Bilton, a manor on the Avon only a few miles upstream from Stratford. Also, the London borough of Stratford abuts the borough of Hackney where de Vere lived at King's

Edward de Vere, the 17th Earl of Oxford

*Writing in **The Elizabethan Review**, Vol. 4 in 1996, respected author Diana Price noted: "The embellishment over the name depicts the coronet of earldom." It is not to be confused with the royal crown.*

Place during the last decade of his life.)

The case for Edward de Vere is intriguing and compelling. The numerous parallels between the author's life and incidents in the plays are undeniable. "William Shakespeare" was the author of the plays and sonnets, but it is apparent from the accumulated evidence that it was a pseudonym for Edward de Vere.

Henry Peacham, one of the most astute literary observers of the era, listed the most "remarkable wordsmiths" and "refined wits" of England's "Golden Age" in his 1622 *The Compleat Gentleman*. Seven names appear – writers "whose likes are hardly to be hoped for in any succeeding age: **Edward, the Earl of Oxford**, Lord Buckhurst, Henry Lord Paget, Philip Sidney, Edward Dyer, Edmond Spenser, and Samuel Daniel."

But no William Shakespeare!

Peacham never "corrected" this "omission" in any of the subsequent editions of his book, which appeared in 1627, 1634 and 1661. The implication is clear – Henry

Shakspere's Signatures

The only examples of William of Stratford's hand writing are six signatures. All are on legal documents, no two of which are alike. The last three are on his will. Note the different spellings – hardly the script of a great writer.

Shakp, 1612, Belott-Mountjoy Deposition

Shakspe(r), 1613, Gatehouse Conveyance

Shaksper, 1613, Gatehouse Mortgage

Shakspere, 1616, first and second sheet of will

Shakspeare, 1616, third sheet of will

Stratfordians have never been able to explain why their candidate could not even write his own name.

(Note: There is evidence that those "signatures" were made by clerks, not by Will himself. See Matt Hutchinson, "The Slippery Slope of Shakspere's 'Signatures,'" *The Oxfordian* 23 [2021], 81)

Peacham knew that the Earl of Oxford and William Shakespeare were one and the same.

No Stratfordian has been able to explain their candidate's comprehensive knowledge of classical literature, as well as Italian and French writers whose works had never been translated into English. The only libraries were in the great houses and were not available to the public – certainly not to the likes of an obscure commoner like Will Shakspere.

Shakspere may well have been illiterate (certainly his parents and his two daughters were). The only examples of his reputed writing are six scrawled signatures on legal documents and all are different, with different spellings of his name. There is absolutely nothing to connect his name to the plays in his lifetime and no mention of a single book or manuscript in his exhaustive will.

No one in Stratford ever referred to *Will Shakspere* as *William Shakespeare* until long after his death. Will Shakspere never claimed that he had written the plays, nor did any of his family. In fact, no one ever

Hedingham Castle was built in the 12th century and was the seat of the de Vere family for over 500 years. It was where Edward de Vere, the 17th earl of Oxford, was born in 1550. The keep (the central tower of any fortified castle) is the only part of the original complex still standing.

The castle is "the best preserved Norman keep in England." It is located in the village of Castle Hedingham, Essex. Although it is a family home, the keep is open to the public from Easter to October.

thought of him as a writer of any sort or even anyone special. His name appears in various accounts for tax delinquency in London and lawsuits over piddling amounts. But there is not a single reference to him as an author.

However, he did manage to gain wealth in excess of anything he could have possibly earned as an actor, playwright, or even as a theatrical entrepreneur.

In contrast, Edward de Vere was special. He was born in 1550 at Hedingham Castle in Essex, the de Vere family seat for over five hundred years. The de Veres had been prominent in English history since the days of William the Conqueror. Edward's father, John de Vere, loved theatrical productions and funded an acting troupe known as Oxford's Men.

When Edward was eleven years old, Queen Elizabeth visited Hedingham Castle for several days. She was apparently enthralled by the revelry and theatrical performances given in her honor. It was perhaps this experience that captured young Edward's attention and to which he would commit his talents for the rest of his life.

Queen Elizabeth I (1533-1603)
Elizabeth Tudor was the daughter of Henry VIII (1491-1547) and his second wife Anne Boleyn, whom he had beheaded for treason in 1536. (He had four more wives after that!) Elizabeth became Queen of England and Ireland in 1558 shortly after the death of her half-sister Mary Tudor, a Catholic known as "Bloody Mary," and ruled until her own death in 1603. "Good Queen Bess" never married so she was the last of the Tudor line. Her successor was James Stuart, James VI of Scotland, who became James I of England.

*The queen was once courted by a Frenchman (a **Frog**), the Duc d'Alençon. He called her his **Little Mouse**. The children's song **The Frog Went A-Courtin'** tells us "… he courted a mouse and her name was **Bess**."*

2 EDWARD'S EARLY YEARS

Young Edward's tutors saw to it that he was grounded in the basic responsibilities of someone of his rank. His principal tutor from the time he was four or five years old was Sir Thomas Smith (c.1513-1577). A Greek orator at twenty, Sir Thomas held the Regius Chair of Civil Law at Cambridge University. He was also provost of Eton College and a member of the Privy Council. Edward spent much of his formative years in Sir Thomas's charge. In addition to Latin, Greek, Italian and French, the rigorous curriculum included the study of writing and drawing, art, ancient history, music, cosmology, dancing, horticulture, astronomy and even medicine. Young Edward was evidently an extraordinary student with curiosity about every facet of life.

When Edward was twelve years old his father died. His mother remarried soon after and, by ancient feudal law, the minor child of a deceased nobleman became a ward of the crown. The young earl entered the household of Sir William Cecil, Queen Elizabeth's

Sir William Cecil (1520-1598) was Queen Elizabeth's trusted advisor and the most powerful man in England.

When his father died in 1562, young Edward became Cecil's ward and was raised in his household. The queen elevated Cecil to the nobility as Baron Burghley in early 1571 so his daughter Anne would be of high enough social status to marry Lord Edward in December 1571. Edward was twenty-one and Anne was only fifteen.

Even many Stratfordians concede that Shakespeare satirized Lord Burghley as Polonius in Hamlet. *Polonius was not an admirable character. It's no wonder Burghley didn't approve of the plays.*

advisor and the most powerful man in the land. He had enormous wealth and a stately mansion with an unrivaled library. The collection included many works by continental writers that had not yet been translated into English but were often referenced throughout the Shakespeare plays.

As a teenager Edward was granted degrees from Cambridge and Oxford and then, at the age of seventeen, enrolled at Gray's Inn, England's premier college of law. He was popular at court and was a favorite of the queen. Edward excelled at sports only played by the aristocracy: He was an avid tennis player, falconer, swordsman and was also a champion at the jousts.

(And the queen delighted in his dancing.)

When he was in his teens, Edward started writing poetry, skits and plays for the court. The Shakespeare plays reflect the author's intimate knowledge of court life – intrigues and even gossip. Many members of the inner circle were satirized in the plays, but the queen approved of and actually supported de Vere's efforts.

Richard Paul Roe makes a convincing case in The Shakespeare Guide to Italy *that the setting for* The Tempest *was the small volcanic island Vulcano just north of Sicily. Roe called it "Prospero's Island."*

3 MARRIED LIFE

In December, 1571, when Edward was twenty-one years old, he married Anne Cecil, who was only fifteen at the time. It was not a happy marriage – one of social and political ambition arranged by Sir William Cecil. In early 1571 the queen raised Cecil's social status to Baron Burghley so his daughter could marry into the nobility. At twenty-one, Edward was no longer Cecil's ward, but he was now his son-in-law. The young man was not enthusiastic about married life. His virtual child bride had always been like a "kid sister," having grown up with Edward in the same household.

So as an adventurous young man in 1575, Edward decided to visit Italy and see for himself the artistic, theatrical and literary center of what came to be known as the Italian Renaissance. As a high ranking aristocrat he was welcomed into the inner circles of the social, intellectual and artistic community.

This sojourn was a seminal experience in de Vere's life as ten of the Shakespeare plays are based in Italy.

Venus and Adonis by Titian (c.1489-1576) (detail)

Titian was the most important painter of the Venetian school. He painted several versions of *Venus and Adonis*. The one in Madrid's Prado and another in the National Gallery in Washington DC depict Adonis bareheaded. The one in Titian's own Venice studio in 1575 was the *only* version showing Adonis with a hat – a "bonnet."

William Shakespeare's 1593 poem *Venus and Adonis* describes Adonis wearing "a bonnet [that] hides an angry brow." Mark Anderson notes that "… all classical sources depict the couple's affair as mutually passionate. Titian's Venus nearly falls over herself to restrain Adonis from leaving." Shakespeare "boldly revises the Ovidian myth in the same way that Titian does."

(Version with bonnet in Galleria Nazionale d'Arte, Antica, Rome.)

Edward de Vere spent several months in Venice in 1575-1576 and ten of the Shakespeare plays are set in Italy. Coriolanus, Titus Andronicus *and* Julius Caesar *were all set in ancient Rome. So some people say that thirteen of Shakespeare's plays were set in Italy.*

But his adventures were not just cultural. On his way back to England from Italy de Vere was captured by pirates. Hamlet wrote to Horatio that he was attacked by pirates and he "alone became their prisoner."

When he returned home he had lost some favor with the queen and the court no longer held the same attraction that it once did. His literary efforts took a prominent place in his life.

De Vere established a household in London which was known as Fisher's Folly. He gathered around him a group of talented writers called the "University Wits." This has led some academics to conclude that the works were not the creation of just one person, Shakespeare, but were somehow a collaborative effort by a team of skillful writers.

There may be some truth to this, but there is no question that the plays were conceived, written and edited by the incredibly gifted author of the works.

In 1586 Queen Elizabeth awarded Edward an annual grant of £1,000 (a huge sum in those days). There were no conditions attached to the annuity.

Richard Paul Roe noted in *The Shakespeare Guide to Italy* that the Villa Foscari/Malcontenta was the prototype for Portia's villa in *The Merchant of Venice*. Shakespeare (de Vere) places Portia's villa "Belmont" on the bank of a waterway (The Brenta Canal) exactly five miles from the Tranect (at Fusina) where the canal boats transfer to the Venice Lagoon. Then another five miles across the lagoon to the Ducal Palace in Venice.

Note: 5 + 5 = 10 x 2 = 20 thus conforming precisely to Portia's statement that …

"we must measure twenty miles today."

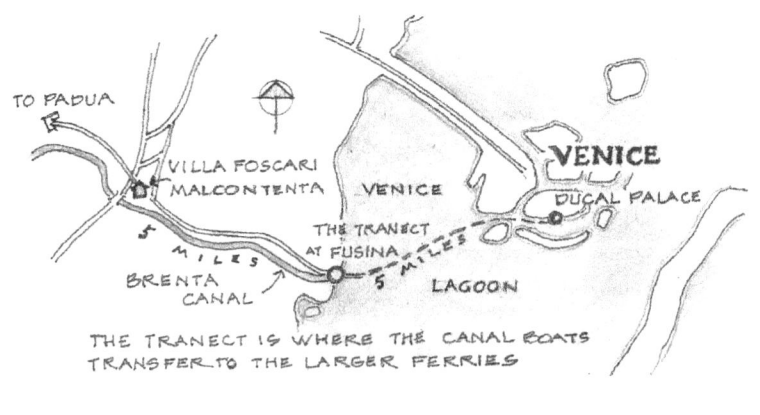

The Villa Foscari pictured above was designed by Palladio. Andrea Palladio (1508-1580) was perhaps the most influential architect in history informing the entire Georgian era in Britain and America.

De Vere subsequently dedicated his life to his literary pursuits. As an aristocrat he could not have published his poems, let alone theatrical works, under his own name. Not only would it have been unseemly, but even dangerous, given the political climate of the times. He skewered many powerful people with impunity – those he called the courtly "reptilia" – as he was always protected by the queen. It was one reason he was resented by some of his peers and especially by his father-in-law.

This was a violent age: duels were common and property was subject to confiscation. Status, and even lives were forfeit, for what today seem like relatively minor offenses. Incarceration in the Tower was an ever-present threat for perceived infractions. Even decapitated heads of executed criminals were mounted on posts along London Bridge! Francis Walsingham, the "Spy-master," and Lord Burghley and his son Robert Cecil, controlled the powerful authoritarian state. All publications were subject to censorship by the Privy Council's enforcer, the Royal Commission.

HAMLET and the Spanish Armada (1588)

Hamlet was a story based on an old Danish tale, but Edward de Vere rewrote it when he was a young man and revisited it in 1587 in anticipation of the invasion of England by the Spanish King Philip II. The Spanish were Catholic and wanted to conquer the Protestant Queen Elizabeth and return her country to the Church of Rome.

Mary Stuart, Queen of Scots, had been a captive of the Elizabethan state since 1568. She was a Catholic and was a threat to Elizabeth's legitimacy as the sovereign of England. Mary had abdicated her claim to the Scottish throne in favor of her son James Stuart. After almost twenty years under Elizabeth's confinement, Mary was executed in February 1587. This event triggered Philip of Spain's aborted attempt to conquer England.

The following passage from Hamlet notes that there was a desperate rush to build a naval fleet to withstand the attack.

The Spanish Armada of 130 ships set sail in 1588 but failed in its attempt. England remained sovereign and Protestant.

Here's a passage from the play:

> *So nightly toils the subject of the land*
> *And why such daily cast of brazen canon*
> *And foreign mart for implements of war*
> *Why such impress of shipwrights whose sore task*
> *Does not divide the Sunday from the week.*
> *What might be toward that sweaty haste*
> *Doth make the night joint laborer with the day*

A possible lost early version of Hamlet *by a young Edward de Vere, called* Ur-Hamlet, *has sometimes been attributed to Thomas Kyd or others by academics because it was too early to fit the traditional narrative.*

4 EDWARD'S LATER LIFE

De Vere sold Fisher's Folly in 1588. Two other things happened that year: The greatly feared Spanish Armada failed in its attempt to conquer England and Edward's wife Anne died at the age of thirty-one. Their three daughters, Elizabeth, Bridget and Susan, were then raised by their grandfather, Lord Burghley.

In 1591 Edward married Elizabeth Trentham, a maid of honor to the Queen, and they soon settled in King's Place in Hackney with over 250 acres of land. (Remember that Hackney abuts the London borough of Stratford.) Elizabeth and Edward had a son Henry, who became Edward's heir, the 18th Earl of Oxford.

In 1593 the name "William Shakespeare" first appeared in print with the publication of the poem **Venus and Adonis** and another, **Lucrece,** the following year. The author's name did not appear again until 1598, following the death of Lord Burghley. As many as a dozen of the Shakespeare plays were performed in the public theaters during the late 1580s and the 1590s without attribution.

Map of central London in the 16th Century
The adjacent boroughs Hackney and Stratford are two miles north of the City

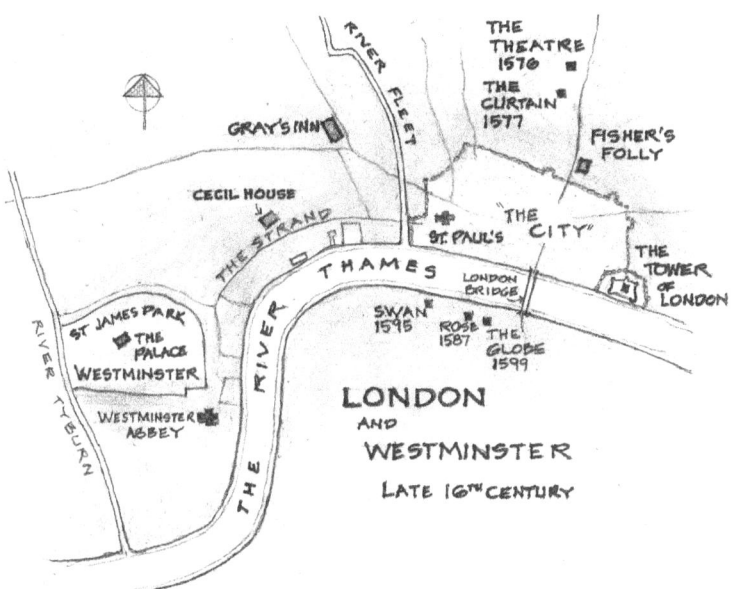

Central London consists of two areas: The City of London, called "The City," with St. Paul's Cathedral within the walls of the old city, and the City of Westminster, with Westminster Abbey about two miles to the west. They were then, as they are now, part of greater London.

The first theaters were built outside of the City walls. James Burbage's The Theatre, 1576, the first successful commercial London theater, and the Curtain, were built north of the City. The Swan, the Rose and later the Globe were built on the south side of the Thames.

Elizabethan/Jacobean London was a filthy, plague-ridden place. In 1666 The Great Fire of London consumed most of the city. The rebuilding was coordinated by architect Sir Christopher Wren. His era of Renaissance classical architecture was sometimes called the "Wrenaissance."

Many of these plays were potentially treasonous, but Will Shakspere was never summoned before the Privy Council's Royal Commission. And one might ask why Shakespeare's plays were exempt from the book burning following the Bishop's Ban in 1599.

By 1597, Will Shakspere had accumulated sufficient funds, supposedly from his involvement in the theater world of London, to buy the "second largest house in Stratford." It was called New Place. He evidently divided his time between his Stratford home and London for a few years before retiring from his various London business ventures. Will Shakspere died in 1616 without anyone taking notice of his death – and certainly not remembering him at the time as any kind of writer or, in fact, anyone distinguished in any way.

Edward de Vere died in 1604, a year after the death of Queen Elizabeth, and the year after King James VI of Scotland became James I of England. The new king loved Shakespeare's plays and had them performed many times in the early years of his reign.
(He also continued Elizabeth's annual grant to Oxford.)

James Stuart, James VI of Scotland (1567-1625), was Elizabeth's successor. He became James I of England upon her death. (His reign was known as the Jacobean era.) James continued to provide Edward with Elizabeth's £1,000 annual grant.

James's son Charles I succeeded his father but was beheaded in 1649. Parliament ruled under Oliver Cromwell until the Restoration of Charles II in 1660. The Stuart dynasty lasted until Queen Anne died in 1714. (The Georgian era followed until Victoria was crowned in 1837)

5   AFTER EDWARD'S DEATH

Several plays written by "William Shakespeare" did not appear in print until long after 1604, the year Edward died. Many Stratfordians believe that they had to have been written shortly before the year of their publication and therefore de Vere could not have been the author.

But when the **First Folio** of thirty-six plays was published in 1623, the canon included eighteen plays that had never been published before. The ten Italian plays revealed extensive knowledge of the geography, customs, art and literature of that country, which was the cradle of the Renaissance. These plays were a critical part of the English Renaissance which evolved during the Stuart dynasty (1603-1714).

"Shake-speares Sonnets" were not published until 1609. The author was noted in the dedication page as "ever-living," a term generally referring only to people who had died.

"SHAKE-SPEARES SONNETS" London 1609

> TO.THE.ONLIE.BEGETTER.OF.
> THESE.INSVING.SONNETS.
> Mr. W. H. ALL.HAPPINESSE.
> AND.THAT.ETERNITIE.
> PROMISED.
>
> BY.
>
> OVR.EVER-LIVING.POET.
>
> WISHETH.
>
> THE.WELL-WISHING.
> ADVENTVRER.IN.
> SETTING.
> FORTH.
>
> T. T.

The dedication on page two of "Shake-speares Sonnets"
Henry Wriothesley, the third earl of Southampton, is generally recognized as the "Fair Youth" in the Sonnets. Anyone who thinks a reputed actor from a provincial town – or anyone connected to the public theaters – could possibly address a high ranking nobleman in intimate and affectionate terms, does not comprehend the rigid class system of the Tudor/Jacobean era.

Final thoughts:

When you hear of a controversy about any subject, don't be quick to embrace one side or the other just because there has been a popularly held theory for even a long time. Whether it's science, biography or almost any commonly held belief, be skeptical. Don't forget that everyone once believed that the earth was flat and that the sun revolved around the earth. Bias can cause a person to adamantly defend a position even in the face of contrary evidence. Don't let pre-conceived ideas learned from "authorities" determine your beliefs. Prominent "experts" often fail to substantiate their opinions with documented evidence. Hearsay is not accepted in a court of law nor should it be the basis for our convictions. Delve into all subjects and theories with an open mind and then – and only then – decide for yourself what makes the most sense.

For many years the Stratfordian claim held sway. But thanks to J. Thomas Looney's landmark book, *"Shakespeare" Identified*, many people in the last one

NOTHING IS TRUER THAN TRUTH

Coat of Arms of Edward de Vere,
the 17th Earl of Oxford
The boar was the heraldic device of the earls of Oxford.

hundred years have come to doubt the conventional notion that the Stratford man was the actual poet/playwright.

There has been a growing "DoubtAboutWill" movement on the Internet with the Shakespeare Authorship Coalition's "Declaration of Reasonable Doubt." Consequently, more and more people from a wide range of disciplines embrace the compelling evidence presented by the writers referenced on pages 34 and 35 and are convinced that……

Edward de Vere, the 17th Earl of Oxford,

was the real

William Shakespeare

Timeline of Edward de Vere's Life

1550 – Edward de Vere is born at Hedingham Castle, the de Vere family seat in Essex, England, since the 12th century.

1555 – Edward is tutored by Sir Thomas Smith until 1562. (Smith was a scholar, Parliamentarian and diplomat.)

1558 – Elizabeth Tudor (1533-1603) becomes queen shortly after the death of her half-sister Mary Tudor, a Catholic known as "Bloody Mary." England is Protestant once again under Elizabeth.

1562 – Edward's father, John de Vere, the 16th Earl of Oxford, dies. Edward becomes a ward of the State and is raised in the household of Sir William Cecil. The same rigorous study program as Smith's continues largely under Arthur Golding, Cecil's brother-in-law.

1564/7 Edward is honored with degrees from both Oxford and Cambridge and is enrolled in Gray's Inn in 1567 to begin his study of law.

1571 – Queen Elizabeth elevates Sir William Cecil's social status. She names him Baron Burghley in early 1571 so his daughter Anne could marry into the nobility. Edward and Anne married in December.

1575/6 Edward spends several months in Italy. Ten of his plays are set in Italy. His specific knowledge of Italian geography has been demonstrated by Richard Paul Roe's *The Shakespeare Guide to Italy*. It is evident that "Shakespeare" had traveled in Italy and his knowledge is revealed in the plays.

1576/7 James Burbage's The Theatre opened. It was the first successful commercial London theater -- followed the next year by The Curtain.

1580 – Edward establishes "Fisher's Folly" and supports the "University Wits." (He sold Fisher's Folly in 1588)

1586 – Queen Elizabeth awards de Vere an annual grant of £1,000 for his lifetime. (There were no conditions attached to this annuity.)

1588 – The Spanish Armada is defeated and Lady Anne Vere dies leaving three daughters, Elizabeth, Bridget and Susan, in Burghley's care.

1590s As many as a dozen "Shakespeare" plays are performed in the theaters without attribution.

1591 – Edward marries Elizabeth Trentham. The couple settle in Hackney, a London borough adjacent to the borough of Stratford.

1593 – Son Henry, the future 18th Earl of Oxford, is born.

1593 – *Venus and Adonis* published with the author noted as "William Shakespeare" for the very first time.

1598 – Burghley dies and the name "William Shakespeare" first appears as the playwright of *Love's Labor's Lost*.

1599 – The Globe theater is built south of the Thames. The Rose (1587) and The Swan (1595) predated it.

1603 – Queen Elizabeth dies and James VI of Scotland becomes James I of England. James continues Elizabeth's annual £1,000 grant to de Vere.

1604 – Edward de Vere dies at King's Place in Hackney – In her 1612 will, his widow requested that she be buried near her husband "in the Church of Hackney."

1609 – "Shake-speares Sonnets" by the "ever-living poet" are published posthumously.

1623 – First Folio included thirty-six plays but eighteen were published for the first time. Ben Jonson's introduction is the first time anyone hinted that the "Sweet Swan of Avon" just might mean that William of Stratford was the author of the plays. But Jonson never mentioned either Shakespeare or Shakspere by name.

NOTE:
The Shakespeare Birthplace Trust published a book titled
Shakespeare Beyond Doubt
(Cambridge University Press, 2013)
Stanley Wells, CBE, Honorary President, Shakespeare Birthplace Trust stated:

> "I have never seen the slightest reason to doubt his [Mr. Shakspere's] authorship." (September 2007)

The Shakespeare Authorship Coalition found this book to be so biased and factually inaccurate that it produced a response:

SHAKESPEARE Beyond Doubt?- Exposing an Industry in Denial
Tamarac FL: Llumina Press, 2013

"… this book may help to dispel some of the negative impressions and untruths being spread about authorship skeptics by the Shakespeare Birthplace Trust of Stratford-upon-Avon."
- Mark Rylance, Artistic Director (1995-2005), Shakespeare Globe Theatre

Diana Price's ***Shakespeare's Unorthodox Biography: New Evidence of an Authorship Problem*** (Westport CT: Greenwood Press, 2001) does not make the case for de Vere – or anyone else – but demonstrates that the author could not have been Will Shakspere.

For a fun and insightful commentary watch:
www.youtube.com/KeirCutler/IsShakespeareDead?

Canadian actor and scholar Keir Cutler, Ph.D., based this YouTube performance on Mark Twain's
Is Shakespeare Dead?

This 2023 book rates Five Stars:
Elizabeth Winkler. *Shakespeare Was a Woman and Other Heresies. How Doubting the Bard Became the biggest Taboo in Literature.* New York: Simon & Schuster, 2023

Some Oxfordian Writers

Looney, John Thomas. *"Shakespeare" Identified in Edward de Vere the Seventeenth Earl of Oxford.* Cary NC: Veritas Publications, (Centenary Edition, James A. Warren, Editor), 2018.

Ogburn, Jr., Charlton. *The Mysterious William Shakespeare: The Myth and the Reality.* New York: Dodd, Mead & Company, 1984

Whalen, Richard. *Shakespeare: Who Was He? The Oxford Challenge to the Bard of Avon.* Westport CT: Praeger Publishers (Greenwood Publishing Group), 1994.

Anderson, Mark. *"Shakespeare" by Another Name: The Life of Edward de Vere, Earl of Oxford, the Man Who Was Shakespeare* New York: Gotham Books (Penguin Group, Inc.), 2005.

Whittemore, Hank. *100 Reasons Shake-speare was the Earl of Oxford.* Somerville MA: Forever Press, 2016.

Cutting, Bonner Miller. *Necessary Mischief: Exploring the Shakespeare Authorship Question.* Jennings LA: Minos Publishing Company, 2018.

Hart, Michael H. *The 100 – A Ranking of the Most Influential Persons in History.* New York: Kensington Publishing, 1992 Number **31**. *EDWARD DE VERE better known as "William Shakespeare" 1550-1604.*

These writers refer to "Shakespeare" simply as the author.

Roe, Richard Paul. *The Shakespeare Guide to Italy*. New York: HarperPerennial (HarperCollins Publishers), 2011

Twain, Mark. *Is Shakespeare Dead?* From *My Autobiography* 1909. San Bernardino CA: 2017.

Audio:

Kreiler, Kurt. *Anonymous Shakespeare – The Man Behind* MP3–CD Performed by Mark Boyett Grand Haven MI: Brilliance Audio.

POSTSCRIPT   Some speculative ideas to ponder

In stating the case for Edward de Vere as the real William Shakespeare, I have endeavored to present information that is convincingly documented by the writers on pages 34 and 35. Undoubtedly there will be challenges to some points, but that's what is so intriguing about this literary whodunit.

Two questions inevitably arise: How did Will Shakspere become William Shakespeare? and Why didn't the First Folio name Oxford as the author?

When did Will Shakspere become William Shakespeare?

In her blog politicworm.com, Stephanie Hopkins Hughes asked: "How did Shak-es-pyeer turn into Shakespeare?" No one knows for certain, but she suggests that Richard Field, who printed *Venus and Adonis* in 1593, *may* have told Oxford about one William Shakspere. He *may* have suggested "a little coin from Oxford to Field and Field to Will and the deal was done." True? Who knows? But it seems as reasonable an explanation as anything I have heard to date.

Alex McNeil, editor of *The Shakespeare Oxford Newsletter*, wrote: "Admittedly, Oxfordians are not in agreement about the details, especially when the plans were first laid. But to me, Shakspere got two things out of this: money and status."

Money: "The price Shakspere paid for New Place was far more than he ever would have made from playwriting and being a share-holder in a theater company. He later was able to buy some tithes in Stratford for another large sum."

So was Stratford paid off? If "coin" closed the deal it must have required the straw man – and his family – to *never* claim any connection to "the works." If that was part of the deal, Will Shakspere honored his side of the bargain.

Status: "In 1596, he finally gets a coat-of-arms for his father, John Shakspere. (something his father had once tried for unsuccessfully.) He can now be called 'Wm. Shakspere, Gent.' – That was a big deal."

In *Every Man Out of His Humour,* Ben Jonson surely had Shakspere in mind when his buffoonish clown Sogliardo brags

"I can write myself a gentleman now. It cost me thirty pounds, by this breath." Puntarvolo suggests "Let the word [motto] be 'Not without mustard' Your crest is very rare, sir."

Shakspere's motto was *supposedly* "Non Sans Droict" ("Not Without Right"). It may very well have been "No, without Right" meaning that John Shakspere had *No Right*. The comma makes a big difference. Evidently Shakspere's pretensions were ludicrous.

Why didn't the First Folio name Oxford as the author?
A quick search on the Internet and you will find no end of speculation. Stephanie Hughes's blog invites inquiry into the many questions that are often unanswerable.

But her critical insight that the opening of James Burbage's The Theatre in 1576 was a seminal innovation. For the first time, dramatic productions were available to the paying public. Indeed, there had been revels, entertaining skits and performances for the inner circle of the Court, the universities, the great houses and the Inns of Court. But now there was an outlet for "playwrights" to share their innovative ideas on the public stage.

The problem: the upper classes and the "authorities" – Burghley and his ilk – viewed this new milieu not just as frivolous and disreputable, but as dangerous, and even evil. No one in the upper ranks dared admit to participating in this sinful activity. This world was comparable to today's underworld of the Mob, drug lords, pimps, prostitutes, and human traffickers. When no peer of the realm could admit to participating in any activity that lowly people did to earn a living, it's no wonder that creative poets/writers/dramatists from the upper classes hid behind pen names.

So when Oxford's "heirs" decided to publish the works for posterity, they honored his original ruse and ascribed the authorship to "William Shakespeare."

The earl had been an iconoclast in life and there would have been no benefit to the project to name him as the real author even nineteen years after his death. It would only have been an unnecessary distraction.

- *JMB*

PSEUDONYMS

Pseudonyms have been in common use by writers for hundreds of years. It is apparent – at least to Oxfordians – that **"William Shakespeare"** was a pseudonym for Edward de Vere. Think how many writers have become famous but were known only by their pen names.

Who was **George Orwell**? (Eric Arthur Blair). Some others: **Edna St. Vincent Millay** (Nancy Boyd); **O. Henry** (William S. Porter); **J. K. Rowling** (Joanne Rowling); **George Sand** (Amantine Lucile Aurore Duprin); **Ayn Rand** (Alisa Zinovevna Rosenbaum); **Lewis Carroll** (Charles Lutwidge Dodgson); **Dr. Seuss** (Theodore Seuss Geisel); **George Eliot** (Mary Anne Evans); **Mark Twain** (Samuel Langhorne Clemens)

And the list goes on.

Here's a less known writer who should resonate with Shakespeare buffs: Who was **Thomas Kyd**? No, not the contemporary of Shakespeare, but the mystery writer who contributed to Ellery Queen's *Mystery Magazine*. **Thomas Kyd** wrote "hard-boiled murder mysteries" about an ex-boxer named Sam Phelan who became a police officer. The author's real name was:

Alfred Bennett Harbage (1901-1976), professor of English Literature at Columbia and later Cabot Professor of English Literature at Harvard. He was the general editor of *The Complete Pelican Shakespeare* (1969). His favorite mystery writer was an Englishman who wrote under the pen name of **Andrew Garve**. The author's real name was Paul Winterton (1908-2001), and in 1953 he was a founding member of the British Crime Writers Association.

Mark Anderson noted that Dr. Harbage thought that only two Shakespeare plays were written after 1604: The Tempest *and* Henry VIII. *Oxfordian writers explain why these plays were written earlier.*

The Author

John Milnes Baker is an architect and writer. He was a 2018 recipient of the Albert Nelson Marquis Lifetime Achievement Award by Marquis Who's Who in America "as a leader in the field of architecture." A graduate of Middlebury College, Baker received his Masters Degree in architecture from Columbia University.

His book *How to Build a House with an Architect* was first published in 1977 by J. B. Lippincott Company and reissued in an expanded edition by Harper & Row Publishers in 1988.

In 1994, W.W. Norton & Company published his *American House Styles: A Concise Guide*, which has remained in print for over twenty-five years. A new enlarged second edition was published in 2018 by Countryman Press, a division of W.W. Norton.

After reading Charlton Ogburn's *The Mysterious William Shakespeare: The Myth and the Reality,* Mr. Baker found the case for Oxford so compelling that he read all the major books on the subject. He became convinced that the Oxfordians made a persuasive case for Edward de Vere as the real author of the plays and sonnets.

Mr. Baker joined the Shakespeare Oxford Society in 1990 and is a member of the Shakespeare Oxford Fellowship, an "…educational organization dedicated to investigating the Shakespeare authorship question and disseminating the evidence that Edward de Vere, the 17th Earl of Oxford, is the true author of the poems and plays written under the pseudonym 'William Shakespeare'."

www.ingramcontent.com/pod-product-compliance
Lightning Source LLC
LaVergne TN
LVHW021740060526
838200LV00052B/3392